Note to parents, carers and teachers

Read it yourself is a series of modern stories, favourite characters and traditional tales written in a simple way for children who are learning to read. The books can be read independently or as part of a guided reading session.

Each book is carefully structured to include many high-frequency words vital for first reading. The sentences on each page are supported closely by pictures to help with understanding, and to offer lively details to talk about.

The books are graded into four levels that progressively introduce wider vocabulary and longer stories as a reader's ability and confidence grows.

Ideas for use

- Begin by looking through the book and talking about the pictures. Has your child heard this story before?

- Help your child with any words he does not know, either by helping him to sound them out or supplying them yourself.

- Developing readers can be concentrating so hard on the words that they sometimes don't fully grasp the meaning of what they're reading. Answering the puzzle questions at the end of the book will help with understanding.

For more information and advice on Read it yourself and book banding, visit www.ladybird.com/readityourself

Book
Band
4

Level 1 is ideal for children who have received some initial reading instruction. Each story is told very simply, using a small number of frequently repeated words.

Special features:

Opening pages introduce key story words

Large, clear type

Kip jumped into the water.
He helped Tip.

Careful match between story and pictures

Educational Consultant: Geraldine Taylor
Book Banding Consultant: Kate Ruttle

LADYBIRD BOOKS

UK | USA | Canada | Ireland | Australia
India | New Zealand | South Africa

Ladybird Books is part of the Penguin Random House group of companies
whose addresses can be found at global.penguinrandomhouse.com.

ladybird.com

Penguin
Random House
UK

First published 2015
001

Copyright © Ladybird Books Ltd, 2015

Ladybird, Read it yourself and the Ladybird logo are registered or
unregistered trademarks owned by Ladybird Books Ltd

The moral right of the author and illustrator has been asserted

Printed in China

A CIP catalogue record for this book is available from the British Library

ISBN: 978-0-723-29519-8

The Bravest Fox

Written by Ronne Randall
Illustrated by Yi-Hsuan Wu

tree

Kip

log

wood

Tip

rocks

7

Kip and Tip went to the wood.

Tip said, "I am a very brave fox. Are you brave, too, Kip?"

Kip said, "I am a very brave fox, too."

They saw a log.

Tip said, "Can you jump over the log? I can!"

Tip jumped over the log.

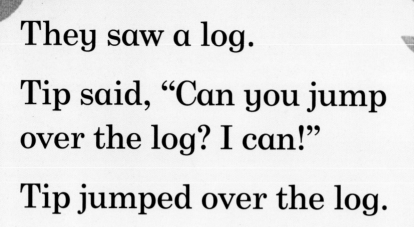

Kip looked at the log.

He could not jump over
the log.

"You are not a very brave
fox," said Tip.

Tip and Kip saw a tree in the wood.

"Can you jump up the tree?" said Tip. "I can!"

Tip jumped up the tree.

"You jump up the tree, too, Kip!" he said.

Kip looked at the tree.

He could not jump up the tree.

Tip said, "You are not a very brave fox, Kip."

Tip and Kip went a
little way in the wood.

They saw a pond.

They saw some rocks
in the pond.

Tip said, "Can you jump on the rocks, Kip? I can. I am a brave fox!"

Tip jumped on the rocks.

Tip went into the water!

"Help me, Kip!" he said.

"I can help you!" said Kip.

Kip jumped into the water.

He helped Tip.

"You are a very brave fox, Kip," said Tip. "You helped me!"

Kip was glad he could help Tip. Tip was glad, too!

How much do you remember about the story of The Bravest Fox? Answer these questions and find out!

- Where are Kip and Tip?

- Which fox can not jump up the tree?

- When does Tip say Kip is a very brave fox?

Look at the pictures from the story and say the order they should go in.

A

B

C

D

Answer: D, C, B, A.

Tick the books you've read!

Level 1

Level 2